nickelodeon

HOUSE OF ANUBIS

The Mask of Anubis

randomhouse.com/kids

ISBN: 978-0-307-98072-4

Printed in the United States of America

10 9 8 7 6 5 4 3 2 1

nickelodeon™
HOUSE OF ANUBIS™

The Mask of Anubis

Adapted by J. E. Bright

Based on the script by Hans Bourlon,
Gert Vehulst, and Anjali Taneja

Random House New York

Nina Martin climbed out of a taxi in front of Anubis House. She wheeled her luggage up to the impressive redbrick building, smiling at its crumbling ivy-covered walls. She was excited to be back at school for a new year after her summer vacation at home in America with her grandmother. Nina couldn't wait to see her friends again. Especially Fabian.

As Nina stepped into the dark front hall, which was decorated with polished wood and ancient Egyptian flair, she could hear people talking in the dining room. She parked her luggage and pushed through a set of double doors deeper inside the house.

"Hey, Nina!" Amber cried. Amber was Nina's pretty blond roommate—sometimes self-absorbed, but funny and charming. She rushed over to hug Nina.

The other students swarmed Nina, welcoming her back.

"Still American?" Patricia, a tall, tart-tongued girl asked, grinning.

"Yep," Nina answered. "Still Patricia?"

Then Nina saw Fabian, who was hanging back from the crowd in his cute, shy way. "Hey!" Nina called to him.

"Hey," Fabian replied, blushing adorably.

Their connection wasn't lost on Amber. "Time to make a discreet exit," she declared.

"Come see our new room, Joy," Patricia told her best friend. Nina didn't know Joy well, as Joy had been away from school most of the previous year. "We share with Mara now."

Sweet and brainy Mara followed Patricia and Joy upstairs, and Amber left too.

Finally alone, Nina went to Fabian and they joined hands, smiling.

"How was your flight?" Fabian asked.

"Good," Nina said. "And you . . . ?"

"I came by car," replied Fabian.

Nina laughed. "Right." She stared awkwardly into Fabian's eyes. They both leaned in for a kiss—

The double doors swung open, and Alfie and Jerome burst in, noisily rushing to the spread of breakfast food on the table.

"Do you mind, *Fabina*?" Jerome said, mockingly combining their names. "People are eating in here, thank you."

After unpacking in her room, Nina headed toward the dark, empty school and made her way to the drama studio, checking that no one else was around. She pried up a loose board on the stage, revealing the gleaming Cup of Ankh hidden inside. She breathed a sigh of relief. The Cup was an ancient Egyptian relic that Nina and her friends had found with the help of an elderly woman named Sarah Frobisher-Smythe.

"Take it," Sarah had told Nina before she died. *"Hide it. Keep it safe."*

At dinner that evening, everyone gathered around the table to enjoy some of housemom Trudy's delicious cooking. Nina sat next to Fabian and squeezed his hand.

"In your last email," Fabian said to Nina, "you

mentioned something about your grandmother coming to visit?"

Nina nodded. "She's staying at a hotel in town. She's really excited to meet you all." She grinned at Fabian. "Especially you. I told her a lot about you."

"Yeah," Patricia joked, "we do breed better geeks over here."

Later that night when the clock chimed ten, Victor Rodenmaar, Anubis House's guardian, made his nightly announcement. "It's ten o'clock," he said. "You have five minutes precisely, and then I want to hear a pin drop!"

That was also the signal for the start of a Sibuna reunion. "Sibuna" was "Anubis" spelled backward, and it was the name of a secret group of students who had gotten involved in the astonishing mysteries of the house.

Nina and Amber met Patricia in the corridor, and they tiptoed toward the attic.

"Do we have anything to pick the lock with?" Amber asked.

With a creak, the attic door slowly swung open by itself. The girls gasped.

"Welcome back to Creepy Towers," said Patricia.

Upstairs, the girls made the Sibuna sign to Fabian and Alfie, lifting a hand to cover one eye. The group had based the sign on a locket that Sarah had given to Nina. It was shaped like the Eye of Horus and could open secret compartments and doors in the house.

After greeting each other, they all sat in a circle. Patricia pulled a newspaper clipping out of her pajama pocket and handed it to Nina. "I thought you guys would be interested in this."

"It's an obituary for Rene Zeldman," said Nina, scanning the clipping.

Rene Zeldman, whose real name was Rufus Zeno, had been a truly dangerous and scary guy who was after the Cup of Ankh hidden in Anubis House. He had been obsessed with Egyptian objects of power, believing he could become immortal with the help of ancient relics.

"Guess he found out the hard way that he wasn't immortal," said Fabian.

Amber stood up, looking for something to cover the dusty floor so she could sit. She yanked a sheet off a bulky object and revealed a big dollhouse. "Ooh," said Amber, bending down to examine it. "I always wanted a dollhouse."

"Even one that's a replica of creepy old Anubis House?" asked Fabian.

Amber stepped back, and they all felt a little spooked.

"Where dollies go to die," murmured Alfie.

Everyone froze when they heard Victor calling. "Come down immediately!" he said.

The students scrambled to hide the dollhouse and rushed down the stairs.

But Nina stayed behind to find a place to stash the Cup of Ankh. With Victor slowly climbing the staircase, calling her name, Nina desperately searched for a good hiding place.

Then the Eye of Horus locket hanging around

her neck started to glow. An Eye of Horus decorating one of the attic walls glowed too, and a secret panel slid open. Grateful, Nina quickly hid the Cup inside and closed the panel. She rushed toward the stairs, bumping into a box in her haste.

Victor appeared just as an old porcelain doll fell out and cracked when it hit the floor.

"Now look what you've done," Victor growled. "Get out!"

Nina rushed past him, but she stopped out of sight on the stairs. She listened as Victor pulled the string on the doll. It spoke in a chilling child's voice, reciting, *"The athenaeum is the place to look. Lift the wings to find the book. Hidden in this book of old: water of life and tears of gold."*

"Water of life," Victor repeated.

Nina sneaked down the stairs.

The next day, Nina and Fabian met up near their lockers in the school hallway. Nina filled Fabian in about the message she'd overheard from the doll. "What's an athenaeum?" she asked.

"Another term for a library," he answered.

Nina smiled warmly. "It's super useful dating a word nerd."

"You can guess what 'water of life' means," Fabian said.

"The Elixir of Life," Nina replied.

Both Victor and Rufus had been seeking one of Anubis House's greatest hidden treasures, the recipe and the means to make an elixir that granted the drinker immortality. But they couldn't make it without the Cup of Ankh, which was now hidden in the attic.

That evening, when Nina headed to dinner, she was surprised to find her grandmother in the hallway talking to Trudy.

"Of course you must stay," Trudy said.

"Gran!" Nina cried. She rushed down and gave her grandmother a big hug. "What's with all the luggage?"

"Just my luck to pick a hotel that floods," Gran replied.

"I thought your grandmother could stay in your room tonight," added Trudy.

Nina smiled. "I'm kind of glad your hotel flooded."

"So am I!" Gran said.

Late in the night, Nina woke from a restless half sleep on the cot set up in her room. A faint, eerie voice called to her.

In a daze, Nina got out of bed and padded into the hallway, heading for the attic. The door opened as Nina approached, and she climbed the stairs in the dark.

"Chosen One," a woman's voice whispered.

Nina stood in the spooky attic, listening, unsure whether she was dreaming.

"How I have waited," the voice whispered in Nina's ear. "You have freed me, Chosen One."

Scared now, Nina turned around and was confronted with a shimmering ghostly presence glowing in the darkness. It was an ancient Egyptian woman, bristling with fierce power. The vision reached out to Nina, revealing dark marks on her palms. Each was the image of a jackal.

Nina backed away. "Who are you?" she gasped. "What do you want?"

"The day will come when everyone will know my name," the specter said. "Find it. Bring it. And you shall weep tears of gold."

"Find what?" asked Nina.

"The Mask of Anubis, child," replied the ghostly woman. "Find it before anyone else!"

She rushed toward Nina until she was frighteningly close, and the woman's eyes sharpened into a chilling glare.

"Or forfeit your life," she hissed.

The next morning, Nina put on her dark red school blazer and reached to the floor for her book bag. She was shocked to see the Cup of Ankh sticking out from under her bed. Nina stuffed it into her bag.

Downstairs in the hallway, Nina showed Fabian the hidden Cup. "It wasn't a dream," she said, her voice trembling. "It was under my bed."

"Maybe you were sleepwalking?" Fabian suggested gently.

Nina shook her head. "The vision mentioned tears of gold. Just like the doll said. It can't be a coincidence."

"Maybe you dreamed it because you heard the doll say it," said Fabian. "We'd better hurry if we don't want to be late for class."

In the science classroom, Fabian sat next to Nina.

He asked, "Was there any mention from Victor's doll about the Mask of Anubis?"

"No, just 'tears of gold,'" she replied. "You think the two are linked?"

The principal, Mr. Sweet, walked into the classroom with Victor close behind. "Before we begin biology," Mr. Sweet said, "I have an important announcement. We have been asked to present an official bid to host a prestigious exhibition."

Victor stepped forward, looking more enthusiastic than normal. "It's the Touring Treasures of Egypt," he explained. "It is absolutely imperative that we win."

"There must be something in that exhibition that Victor wants," Nina whispered to Fabian. Victor had been just as obsessed as Rufus with obtaining the Cup. Now Nina realized he must be after another Egyptian artifact.

"Volunteers to help us prepare the bid should meet at the Frobisher Library this afternoon," Victor said.

Fabian and Nina decided to volunteer so they could see what Victor was looking for. After the meeting ended, Fabian and Nina hung out in the library to do some research.

Fabian held up an exhibition catalog. "Look," he said. "It contains every item that will be in the expo. Maybe we can figure out what Victor is interested in." Then he noticed that Nina didn't have her bag. "Are you still carrying the Cup around?"

"No," she said. "I managed to put it back in the attic. It's safer there." She flipped a page of the reference book she was skimming. "Fabian," she whispered urgently. "Listen. 'The Mask of Anubis was a mythical mask worn by the high priest of Anubis, God of Death. Legend has it that when worn at the funerals of pharaohs, the mask would weep tears of gold.' If Victor is after tears of gold, that means he needs the mask!"

The next morning at breakfast, Fabian pulled out the exhibition catalog again. "I was looking through this last night." He pointed to a picture of a bronze mask.

"The Mask of Anubis," Nina breathed.

"It's a replica," Fabian said. "But you'll never guess who made it. Louisa Frobisher-Smythe!"

Nina's eyes widened in amazement. Louisa was

Sarah's mother. Louisa and her husband, Robert, had founded Anubis House. They were responsible for its ancient Egyptian mysteries.

Victor entered the dining room, and Fabian quickly shut the catalog, which sparked Victor's suspicion. The caretaker confiscated the catalog.

That afternoon, after chatting with Amber and Joy in the girls' restroom, Nina was left alone. A vision of the ghostly Egyptian woman appeared in the mirror, standing behind her. When Nina whirled around, nobody was there.

That night, Nina lay in bed pondering all the clues. Suddenly, there was a knock on the door. Fabian peered into her room.

"Why are you hiding from me?" he asked.

"I'm not," she replied, confused.

"You can't ignore me forever, Nina," Fabian said ominously.

Nina hopped to her feet, irritated. "Who's ignoring you?" she demanded.

Fabian's eyes blazed. "I said you can't ignore me forever!" He grabbed her arm, and his face shifted into that of the female Egyptian spirit, twisted in fury.

Nina gasped, horrified, and pulled away.

"The mask is close; I feel it," the phantom hissed. "Ask the one who knows."

Then she vanished in a flash of blinding light.

4

Nina woke up in bed the next morning confused about whether she'd dreamed the horrible visitation. She glanced down at her arm where the ghostly woman had grabbed her and was shocked to see the same jackal mark that the specter had had on her palms.

It wouldn't come off, no matter how hard Nina rubbed.

Fabian took Nina that morning to visit his uncle Ade's antiques shop so they could probe his knowledge about the mysteries they were discovering. But instead of Uncle Ade, they found a different man in the shop.

"Jasper!" Fabian said happily. "I thought you were in Peru. Where's Uncle Ade?"

"Egypt," Jasper replied. "Archeological dig. I'm shop-sitting as a favor."

Fabian introduced the man to Nina as his god-father. "If anyone's going to know about this weird stuff, it's him," Fabian said. "Total Egypt geek."

"Have you heard of the Mask of Anubis?" asked Nina.

Jasper nodded. As he picked up the shop's copy of the exhibition catalog to show them, Nina said, "We mean the real one. Where do the experts think that one might be?"

"Nobody knows," said Jasper. "There are theories, but now most think the mask was a myth."

Fabian reached over and pulled up Nina's sleeve, showing Jasper the mark on her arm.

Jasper's face paled. "The Mark of Anubis," he whispered. "Mythology suggests that the god Anubis marks those who wrong him as a curse."

"But the spirit wasn't Anubis," said Fabian. "It was a woman."

Jasper shook his head. "I haven't the faintest clue who that would be."

Being marked by the spirit wasn't the only thing Nina had to worry about. By the time she was getting ready for bed that night, she was starting to feel uneasy. Since school had started, Fabian had been spending a lot of time with Joy. Fabian and Joy had been best friends before Nina had arrived at Anubis House, and now Nina was beginning to wonder how close the two of them actually were.

Amber was sitting on her bed, painting her toenails, so Nina confided in her friend. "Fabian and Joy look very cozy together, huh."

"Uh-oh," Amber muttered.

"I hate feeling like this," Nina complained. "I just need to get over it, don't I? I mean, why should a cursed spirit stop me from dating?"

Amber eyes opened wide. "I knew there was stuff you weren't telling me. Does this have to do with the Cup, when it glowed that time? Or our favorite clue-y old lady?"

"Sarah's at rest now," Nina answered, wishing she'd kept quiet. "She can't help us anymore."

Suddenly, Amber pointed across the room. "Look!" she gasped. Alfie had brought the dollhouse from the attic and given it to Amber as a present earlier that day. Now light was pouring out of its windows, and smoke issued from the tiny chimney.

"Does it have batteries?" asked Amber.

Someone knocked on the door. Nina and Amber quickly stood in front of the dollhouse, blocking it from view. But it was just Fabian, so they let him in.

Fabian saw the glowing dollhouse and hurried over to it. "What's it doing?"

Nina inspected the miniature replica and found something surprising written on the back. She turned the house around. "This was Sarah's," she said, showing them the childish printing.

Shivering, Nina stood with the others and watched the dollhouse's windows begin to glow more brightly.

The next afternoon, once Gran had left Anubis House to continue her travels across England, Nina met Fabian in the living room. They sat close together on the sofa, flipping through the exhibition catalog they'd borrowed from Jasper.

"If Sarah's mother made the mask replica," Fabian said, "she must have seen the original at some point. Right?"

"I was thinking the same thing," Nina said. "So . . . what if the Frobisher-Smythes brought back more than just the Cup of Ankh from Egypt?"

Amber entered the living room and plopped herself onto the couch beside Nina. "Hey, what's the goss?" she asked. "Sibuna me."

But Nina didn't want Amber to get involved in something so dangerous, so she changed the subject.

Later that night, Nina was awakened by a glow from the dollhouse. She opened her eyes, watching the light. Then she hurried over to the dollhouse and peered in the windows.

"Sarah, I don't know what you're trying to show me," she said, frustrated.

A hidden drawer in the base of the dollhouse suddenly slid open. Inside was a small, tightly wound scroll.

"Finally!" Nina said.

At breakfast the next morning, Nina waited until everyone else had gone to class before she showed Fabian the scroll she'd found. On it was a hand-drawn map.

"It looks like a sequence of tunnels," Nina said. "And look at this symbol. You think that's where the mask is hidden?"

"The Mark of Anubis," Fabian said with a shudder. His face was creased with worry.

"Hey," Nina asked softly, "what's up?"

"I dreamed about her last night," Fabian admitted. "The spirit."

Horrified, Nina gazed seriously into his eyes. "Did she touch you? Do you have the mark?"

"N-no," he stammered, and quickly focused on the map again. "So if the mask is hidden in tunnels under the house, how do we get to it?"

"Is that what I think it is?" Amber asked from behind them. "A treasure map!"

Before school, while Fabian was busy making a short film for the exhibition bid, Nina and Amber sneaked into the kitchen. Nina held her locket up to an old bread oven, and a secret passageway to the cellar sprang open.

"Want to go first?" she asked.

"After you," said Amber. "And I've decided," she added while Nina was descending a small stairway, "that you and Fabian are coming on a double date this evening with Alfie and me."

Nina gulped. "This evening?"

"Leave it any longer and you guys really will be just friends," Amber insisted.

Down in the gloomy cellar, they found Victor's workbench in its usual spot. The table was covered in vials and beakers, some bubbling and filled with a greenish liquid used for his quest to replicate the elixir of immortality. Nina and Amber crept past it and then followed the map to an area they hadn't explored before.

When they reached a bookshelf built into an alcove, Nina's locket started to glow. One of the shelves had a complicated design carved along the top.

"Look at that pattern of snakes," Nina said.

"Oh," Amber said, "are those snakes? I thought they were eights."

Nina laughed, realizing Amber was right. "You're a genius."

"A genius with perfect hair," added Amber. "Double threat."

Examining the pattern, Nina discovered that four of the carvings in the middle rotated, revealing digits on hidden wheels.

"It's a kind of Victorian combination lock," Nina said. "But what's the code?"

Amber patted her pockets. "I must've left my book of secret Victorian codes upstairs."

Nina ignored her joke. "People use codes that are

easy to remember," she said. "Like birthdays. Sarah's birthday!" She spun the snake wheels until they showed the year of Sarah's birth.

Nothing happened.

"Okay, so it's not Sarah's birthday," said Nina.

"I don't want to rush you," Amber said, "but we were meant to be at school like five minutes ago."

During school, Nina filled Fabian in on what she and Amber had found, and they decided to try both Robert's and Louisa's birth years, as well as the year Anubis House was founded. They would have thought of more numbers, but Amber dragged them out on a picnic with Alfie as soon as school was over.

The date was a total disaster, as Alfie accidentally drove over the picnic spread with a pink lawn mower and crashed into a hedge. Nina and Fabian escaped, preferring to explore the newest mystery.

Unfortunately, back down in the cellar, none of the numbers Nina and Fabian tried unlocked anything.

"I'm stuck," Nina admitted. "I have no idea what the code is."

They fell into a defeated silence until Nina broke

it with an awkward question. "You didn't really want to go on that date, did you?"

"Oh . . . no," said Fabian. "Yeah, no . . . I did. I just—"

Nina flushed, embarrassed that she'd asked. "I didn't either," she said. "I told Amber that you're my best friend. And that's so important to me. I'd do anything to protect that. This boyfriend-girlfriend thing is kind of complicated. . . ."

"So . . . ," Fabian said, "you think we were better off before? When we were just . . ."

"Friends?" asked Nina, feeling frustrated and sick to her stomach. "Why? Is that what you want? What are you trying to tell me?"

After a long, terrible pause, Fabian let out a sad sigh, and offered his hand for her to shake. "Friends it is."

Feeling shocked and numb, Nina shook his hand. "Right," she said miserably.

At the top of the stairs, the cellar door creaked open. "Who's down there?" Victor called.

Before Nina could reset the snake carvings, Victor hurried down the steps. "What's so interesting over there?" he demanded when he saw them. "Move away from that alcove!"

Nina was feeling so terrible about her breakup with Fabian that she couldn't think of an excuse to keep Victor from seeing that the snakes had been moved, revealing hidden numbers.

Then Amber appeared at the top of the stairs. "Victor!" she cried. "There's a weasel in the heating vent! I smell burned weasel!"

Victor headed upstairs to help Amber, and Nina and Fabian quickly turned the snakes back into eights so that the numbers vanished into the pattern.

"Let's get out of here," Nina said sadly.

6

The next afternoon, the school presented its bid to host the Treasures of Egypt exhibition. Fabian's short film about Anubis House and its devotion to the preservation and celebration of Egypt and its treasures was a success, as were the speeches by Joy and Patricia. Despite some disruptive clowning by Alfie in a King Tut outfit, they were awarded the exhibition! It would be hosted in a few weeks in the Frobisher Library, and Trudy was leaving Anubis House temporarily to become the exhibition's new assistant curator, working with Fabian's godfather, Jasper.

That was all good news. Another bit of good news was that during the presentation, Mr. Sweet mentioned the year the Frobisher Library was founded: 1890! Nina thought the year might work as the secret combination they were trying to figure out.

But the news wasn't all good for Nina: to celebrate their winning presentation, Joy gave Fabian a big, lingering hug. Even worse, while Fabian hugged Joy, his shirtsleeve was pushed up, and Nina spotted the Mark of Anubis on his arm. He was cursed too! Nina confronted Fabian after they left the library, and he admitted that he had woken up with the mark after his nightmare about Senkhara.

Later that night, Fabian, Nina, and Amber went down to the cellar to try the new number on the snakes. But first Fabian and Nina showed Amber the marks on their arms.

"Ouch," Amber said. "Matching tattoos. Right before you split up."

"No," Nina said. "It's the Mark of Anubis. It means we have to find the Mask of Anubis for this ancient Egyptian spirit. If we don't, we forfeit our lives."

"Oh, well," said Amber. "At least it's not like you're going to die or anything."

"Amber," Fabian explained, "that's what 'forfeit our lives' means."

Nina pulled down her sleeve. "I didn't want anyone else to get involved, in case they get cursed too."

Amber looked genuinely worried. "I'm trying to deal with the fact that my best friends are totally cursed."

Nina nodded sympathetically. "So here's the deal," she said. "We have to put in the combination and go through that door. . . . But you stay here."

"We can't ask you to take a risk like that for us," added Fabian.

Amber covered one eye with her hand, making the Sibuna sign. "Sibuna," she said firmly.

"Sibuna," Nina and Fabian repeated, making the sign.

They were all in this together. Amber would go too.

Nina strode over to the alcove and turned the snake wheels until they showed the numbers 1-8-9-0. For a tense moment, nothing happened.

Then a bone-jarring grinding sound filled the cellar, and the back of the alcove slid to the side, revealing a secret room beyond it.

Nina, Fabian, and Amber ducked through the

alcove and found themselves in an untidy study with dusty books on the shelves, battered leather sofas, a cluttered writing desk, papers piled on the floor, and framed portraits lining the walls. Everything was coated in cobwebs.

"Seriously," said Amber, "when will we find something that isn't old and crusty?"

They began exploring the mess and located a peephole into the cellar and a button that controlled the door to the alcove.

Amber shrieked. She had touched a portrait of Robert Frobisher-Smythe, and it had fallen off the wall with a crash.

Behind the portrait was a hidden recess where engraved amulets were hanging from chains on pegs. Now they were glowing softly.

"Weird place to keep your jewelry," said Amber.

They arranged the amulets on the desk to inspect them.

"There's a different hieroglyph on each one," Fabian said. "Spider, bird, crocodile—"

"I've seen these before," Nina broke in. She unfolded the map and showed them that each symbol matched a hieroglyph that marked a different room in the tunnels. "But how do these amulets help us? We've hit a dead end."

"We need more research," Fabian said. He turned to a bookcase and grabbed a stack of cobwebby books. "These look like journals." Each was marked with the initials *R.F.S.* on the spine. "They're Robert Frobisher-Smythe's diaries! Why don't we take a few and see if they make any reference to amulets or doorways."

For the rest of the day, Nina and Fabian skimmed the diaries in the dining room. The writing was extremely boring. They had almost given up reading the entries when Amber showed up.

"I've got the lowdown on the amulets," Amber told them. "They were worn for protection . . . against bad luck, danger, or evil spirits."

"How did you find that out?" asked Nina.

"I've always been the brains of Sibuna," Amber replied. When both Nina and Fabian raised their eyebrows in disbelief, she admitted, "Okay, I asked Jasper. He's your godfather, Fabian. We can trust him, right?"

"Yeah," Nina said. "But we still need to be discreet."

In the morning, Nina, Fabian, and Amber went down to the hidden study in the cellar to look for more clues. Nina found a small hole cut into a bookshelf, through which she could see a dingy tunnel beyond. But they didn't know how to open the secret passageway.

While Nina searched the bookshelf for some kind of hidden trigger, Amber inspected the book spines, and Fabian stared at pictures of Robert Frobisher-Smythe.

"There's a symbol of a bird on the top shelf here," said Nina.

Fabian hurried over to the row of amulets on the desk. "I've seen that symbol." He picked up an amulet engraved with a long-legged bird with a curved beak. "It's an ibis, the symbol of Thoth. Thoth is the god of wisdom and learning."

While Nina and Fabian examined the ibis amulet on the desk, Amber said, "I've seen him before, on one of these books." She headed back to the shelf.

"Here," Amber said. "Our crazy fun-time god of moldy old books." She began to pull out a book with an ibis on the spine.

Suddenly, the entire bookshelf revolved, spinning Amber into the tunnel.

"I take it back!" Amber hollered. "Books are awesome! Let me out!"

Behind the wall, Amber saw an intensely bright light shining around the edges of the bookshelf, and she cried out in terror.

Nina and Fabian raced to the shelf, searching for a way to turn it around again.

"What can you see back there?" Fabian called to Amber.

"Nothing!" Amber wailed. "And I mean nothing! There was a big flash of light, and now my eyes don't work!"

"Booby trap," Fabian told Nina grimly.

Amber kicked the bookshelf on her side, and Nina noticed that the top right corner of the shelf moved slightly. She spotted a tiny camouflaged button there.

"Look," Nina said. "Press it!"

Fabian pushed the button.

The bookcase whirled around, spinning Amber back into the study. As soon as the shelf stopped moving, a scratchy recording behind a portrait of Robert Frobisher-Smythe started to play.

"*To those who've trespassed where they do not belong, the beacon of light is your warning song,*" chanted the voice. "*Your eyes shall not see, all shall be dark . . . until Ra completes his blazing arc.*"

"Ra is the sun god," Fabian explained. "He represents the sun's arc from dawn to dusk. Or one full day."

"And I bet the voice on the recording is Robert Frobisher-Smythe. He hid the Cup of Ankh—and probably the Mask of Anubis as well!" added Nina.

"I won't be able to see for a whole day?" Amber moaned.

Fabian shifted Amber to a safe spot and examined the bookshelf again. "You're sure you pulled on the book with Thoth on the spine?"

"I'm sure," replied Amber. "I could actually see back then."

"There must be a way to turn off that trap," said Fabian.

Then Nina noticed that in every portrait of Robert Frobisher-Smythe, he was wearing an amulet! She smiled. "Amber," she asked, "you said amulets were for protection, right? Like . . . maybe protection against booby traps?"

Fabian grinned, and he and Nina each hung an amulet around their necks. They pulled out the book with the ibis symbol on the spine and then spun around with the bookshelf into the dark tunnel.

A harsh beam of light shot out at their feet and climbed their bodies. Fabian nervously took Nina's hand. The beam rose until it hit the amulets on their chests.

Then the beam of light flickered out.

"The amulets worked!" Fabian cheered.

Nina laughed in relief and glanced down at Fabian's hand holding hers.

Fabian let go, blushing. "Sorry," he said.

Fabian and Nina helped Amber down to breakfast in the morning. Amber was wearing huge sunglasses to disguise her temporary blindness. In the dining room, Victor introduced all the students to the temporary new housemom, an elegant blonde named Vera, and he explained that Trudy had already started working on the exhibition.

Later that day, Fabian and Nina returned to the hidden study in the cellar, and, wearing the protective amulets, spun around with the bookshelf to explore the new tunnel. Once again, the blinding beam of light didn't affect them.

In the middle of the tunnel they found an ornate pedestal, which Fabian stopped to examine. Nina continued exploring but found only a locked door with a triangular hollow in the center of it a short distance ahead.

"So we've got a door but no key," said Fabian. "And a pedestal with nothing on it."

Nina strode back along the tunnel to the revolving bookshelf. "We've also got a bookcase full of books," she said. "Now what?"

"Well...," Fabian said thoughtfully, "the bookcase is marked with the symbol for Thoth, the god of knowledge. And we get knowledge from books . . ."

Nina inspected the bookcase more carefully. After poking around, she noticed that there were six similar books on one shelf, each labeled with a letter on its spine. She read the letters out loud. "*R-E-B-T-R-O.* Rebtro."

"I don't get it," said Fabian.

Nina smiled. "It's an anagram. For Robert." She quickly rearranged the books so the letters spelled *R-O-B-E-R-T.*

Then a grinding noise and the sound of whirring cogs echoed through the tunnel from behind the pedestal. Both Nina and Fabian stared expectantly at the pedestal and the distant locked door, but the noises stopped without any changes to the tunnel.

"So . . . ," Nina said, "it's not what's *in* the books; it's what's *on* them. We need to spell his full name."

"And Robert Frobisher-Smythe is definitely a full name," joked Fabian.

They searched the shelves and collected any books that had single letters on the spines, and managed to spell out *S-M-Y-T-H-E.*

But the nine books that would have spelled out "Frobisher" were missing.

"Where could they be?" Nina asked.

"The Frobisher Library?" suggested Fabian. He glanced at his watch. "We can't look now—we're late for class. Let's go."

They pulled out the ibis book to swivel back into the study and were about to open the secret door into the main cellar when they heard voices.

"Wait," Nina whispered. "It's Victor. And the new housemom, Vera."

Nina and Fabian pressed their ears against the door, their foreheads almost touching.

"What an impressive cellar," Vera said.

Victor chuckled in reply.

"What are they doing?" Fabian asked.

"Flirting, I think," Nina replied. She shuddered.

"Maybe Victor's in love," said Fabian.

Fabian and Nina laughed for a second, until they realized how close together they were. They shifted uncomfortably, hyperaware of their own complicated feelings for each other.

"The timepiece, child," a sinister voice whispered in Nina's ear. "Watch the timepiece."

Nina gasped, whirled around, and saw the Egyptian spirit glaring right at her before the ghostly figure vanished.

"Was that her?" Fabian asked softly, concerned.

Nina nodded. "Yeah."

"What did she say?"

"'Watch the timepiece,' whatever that means." Nina's shoulders slumped. "It feels like she's always watching."

Fabian put his arm around Nina, and she rested her head on his shoulder.

At lunchtime the next day, Fabian and Nina visited the Frobisher Library. Trudy was busy dusting old antiquities, so they were able to search the book stacks for any volumes whose spines were marked with only a letter, like the ones in the tunnel. It helped that the books were all from the same series, Fables of Egypt.

It didn't take long for them to find most of the books and stuff them into their bags.

"I found another one," Nina announced.

"Great," Fabian said. "That makes eight! Just one more." He picked up a dusty notebook and started flipping through it. "This is a lending ledger. It dates back to the sixties."

"If someone took out the book back then and didn't return it," Nina said, "then—"

"Big late fee?" Fabian guessed.

"No," Nina said. "We'll never find it!"

Fabian returned his attention to the lending ledger. "Yeah," he said. "Fables of Egypt, volume seven. It was taken out . . . a couple of years ago. By someone called DABEd."

"Is that some quirky British name I haven't heard of before?" Nina asked.

"Don't think so," replied Fabian. "Maybe it's a code word?"

"Okay," Nina said. "So . . . how do we find out who DABEd is?"

After lunch, Nina and Fabian went to Mrs. Andrews' French class. Every time Nina glanced at Fabian, she could tell he was deep in thought. He kept staring at Mrs. Andrews' diploma on the wall.

"Daphne Andrews," Fabian muttered.

Then his eyes lit up.

"Nina," he whispered. "What if DABEd isn't an actual name. . . . What if they're initials? D.A.—Daphne Andrews. And B.Ed.—Bachelor of Education! DABEd."

"Oui," Nina said with a smile.

When class was over, Nina and Fabian enlisted Amber, who had regained her eyesight, to help them search Mrs. Andrews' classroom.

"We just need this last book," Fabian explained.

Amber scoffed. "And you think Andrews took it and left it lying around her classroom for two years?"

Nina was searching the desk, Fabian was checking out the storage closet, and Amber was looking through the window shelves when Mrs. Andrews surprised them by returning to her classroom.

The three students froze and then smiled awkwardly.

Before Mrs. Andrews could say anything, Fabian stepped closer to her. "Mrs. Andrews, may I ask you a question about the Frobisher Library? A very important book has gone missing, and we thought you'd be able to make an announcement about it in class."

Mrs. Andrews blinked at Fabian. "Well, I could," she replied, "but nobody's borrowed a book from there in years."

"It's a book you took out two years ago," said Fabian.

Mrs. Andrews paused, thinking. "I think I know where that book might be. Leave it to me."

The students left, and Nina and Amber met up again later to stake out the library, keeping out of sight as they waited for Mrs. Andrews to return with the book.

"Where's Fabian?" Nina asked.

"He had to go tutor Joy," Amber said. Then she realized what she'd just said. "Or something," she added hastily.

"He's Joy's study buddy now?" Nina asked in a hurt voice.

"Oops," Amber said, wincing. "I was going to break it to you gently."

Then Mrs. Andrews walked by their hiding place, and Nina and Amber followed her at a distance into the library. They ducked in quickly and scooted behind a bookcase, where they saw her hand the book over to Victor.

"What is she doing?" whispered Nina.

"May I ask why you need this book, Victor?" said Mrs. Andrews.

"Research—I'm looking for information about a very important artifact, and I think this might help," Victor replied.

The girls hoped Victor would return the book to the shelves, but instead he headed out with it tucked under his arm. As he went by them, the girls heard him mutter, "This had better help me find the mask!"

Nina gasped. "Victor's after the Mask of Anubis too!"

Before he could leave, Amber leapt out in front of him. "Jasper! Trudy!" she hollered. "Victor's taking something he shouldn't. Call out the dogs!"

Jasper hurried over. "What's going on?"

Victor sneered at Amber. "This ridiculous girl is attempting to prevent me from borrowing this book."

"These books are part of the exhibition now," Jasper said to Victor. "Mr. Sweet's orders. Someone was in here tampering with the boxes yesterday, so we have to be most careful." He held out his hand for the book, and Victor reluctantly gave it to him and strode away.

When Victor was gone, Amber smiled and pulled the book out of Jasper's hands. "I can put that back for you," she offered.

Jasper nodded, and hurried away to resume helping Trudy set up the exhibition.

With all the books in their possession, Nina, Fabian, and Amber met up later that night in the tunnel. They quickly arranged the books on the re-volving bookshelf in the right order. Now the spines spelled out *R-O-B-E-R-T F-R-O-B-I-S-H-E-R S-M-Y-T-H-E.*

As soon as the last book was in place, the pedestal came alive with the whirring of machinery. Its top slid to one side, and a cube slowly emerged from the column.

Fabian rushed over and grabbed the cube. It was elaborately decorated and rattled when he shook it. "Something's inside," he said.

"If it's shiny and expensive, I call dibs," said Amber.

Fabian smiled. "I think it's the key to that door."

"So open the cube!" Nina said.

Fabian twisted the cube until his face turned red, but it wouldn't open, no matter how hard he tried.

8

The next morning at breakfast, the students were introduced to Eddie, a new Anubis House member. Eddie was American and had spiky blond hair and a sarcastic wit. He flirted with the girls and charmed all of them—much to the dismay of the other guys.

During lunch the next day, Nina, Amber, and Fabian gathered in Nina's room to try to solve the mystery of the cube. After turning it with no results, Nina looked despondently at the cube in her hands.

"Here, give it to me," Fabian said. He took the cube and started fiddling with it.

As she watched Fabian grow more frustrated with the cube, Nina heard a loud cracking noise. She spun around to see a line running up the side of the dollhouse and branching out horizontally to meet the front and back eves. She traced a finger along the horizontal crack, then up one gable and down the other. The crack had made a triangle! Nina got an idea. "Here, give it to me!" she told Fabian.

Fabian shook his head. "No, Nina, I've got it."

"Fabian, give it to me!" Nina snatched the cube from his hands and smashed it loudly on the floor.

The door flew open and Victor stormed in. Nina and Fabian took a quick step closer to each other, shielding the broken cube from Victor's view.

"What is going on in here?" thundered Victor. "Home for five minutes and already an almighty commotion!"

Amber jumped in. "A lovers' tiff, Victor. Nina and Fabian are going out. Sorry, *were*."

Nina and Fabian shot Amber outraged looks. But Victor blanched, his anger giving way to embarrassment. "Well, if you must tiff, kindly do it quietly," he said, withdrawing hastily.

As soon as Victor left, Nina and Fabian turned their attention to the broken pieces of the cube. Fabian held up a small diamond-shaped jewel.

"Interesting!" he murmured. Meanwhile, Nina had started to reassemble the cube.

"What are you doing?" Amber asked.

"The dollhouse cracked and made a triangle. So I cracked the cube. And made a triangle." Nina held up the pyramid she had made with the cube pieces.

Fabian handed Nina the jewel and she fit it snugly on top of the pyramid. Nina smiled triumphantly. "We should go check out the tunnels tonight."

Later that night, while the other students slept, Nina, Fabian, and Amber stole down into the cellar. After putting on their amulets and navigating past the blinding beam of light, they went to the door at the end of the secret passageway. Nina held the pyramid up to the door, and the triangular hollow in the center of the door started to glow. When she slid the pyramid into the hollow, the door opened with a loud grinding sound.

Beyond the door was another tunnel. "Shall we see what's inside tunnel number two?" Nina asked excitedly.

The Sibuna members followed the tunnel around

a bend. Suddenly, Amber stepped one foot over the edge of a chasm. She lost her balance, almost toppling headfirst into a pitch-black abyss.

Fabian and Nina grabbed Amber and pulled her back just as a small stone tumbled over the edge. The three students listened as the stone dropped through the darkness until they finally heard a very distant *plop* into water. "Wow, that was close," breathed Amber.

"There must be some way to get across," said Fabian. He pointed to something on the far side of the chasm. "What's that?"

A small, pointed jetty stuck out from the chasm's edge. They saw a similar jetty on their side as well.

"It looks like something goes over there," said Nina. She studied the rock wall that was twelve feet behind them, where a tall wooden beam was nestled against it. "Look! I bet this is our bridge!"

"There must be a button or a lever or something to make it go across this abyss," said Fabian.

Nina examined the beam. "This is carved into a shape. It looks like a crocodile—like the one on the hieroglyph!" She spotted a small cavity at the base of the wall. "Here's something!" she called.

Nina and Fabian got down on their hands and knees and peered into the cavity. It was deep, with something set at the front that looked like teeth.

"It's like a crocodile jaw," said Fabian.

Nina craned her neck to look farther inside. "I see something. It looks like a lever!"

Fabian gingerly slid his hand into the cavity and felt the lever. The crocodile teeth suddenly clamped shut on his arm, and he cried out in pain. The jolt made him pull the lever by mistake! There was a click, and the crocodile-shaped beam fell away from the wall—heading straight for Amber.

Amber screamed. She dived out of the way as the crocodile beam came crashing down, barely missing her as it hit the ground with a resounding thud.

After prying Fabian's arm out from the crocodile's teeth, the three Sibuna members tried to pick up the beam.

"This thing weighs a ton," groaned Fabian.

Nina shook her head in despair. "There's no way we're going to get that to the edge, let alone over the chasm. It'd take four men to lift."

A conspiratorial look came across Amber's face. "How about three girls and two men? Well, boys."

Fabian and Nina looked at her, both knowing exactly what she meant. Patricia and Alfie were Sibuna members too. Perhaps working together, the five of them could move the beam!

"It's time to get the gang back together!" declared Amber.

9

The next day, all five Sibuna members gathered in the living room. Nina and Amber filled in Patricia and Alfie on the new mysteries they had discovered, including their latest problem, while Fabian buried his head in a notebook, pen frantically scribbling diagrams.

After some time, Fabian looked up with a smile. "Okay, I think I've worked it out. We rig a counterweighted boom system that lifts up the beam and sets it in place."

The Sibuna members all looked at him blankly.

"What?" asked Fabian.

"Why don't we just lift the beam on its end and drop it over the chasm?" asked Amber nonchalantly. Nina, Patricia, and Alfie nodded.

Fabian's grin faded. "Yeah, that . . . that could work too," he admitted.

🐦

In the dark stillness of the night, the Sibuna members gathered around the crocodile beam. After some heaving, they got it upright, swaying at the lip of the chasm. The beam was tapered at each end, and they struggled to keep it standing up straight. Finally, they maneuvered the beam into the perfect position.

"Okay, guys, let it go!" cried Nina.

They all released the beam and leapt back from the edge. With a *clunk,* the beam hit the jetty on the far side dead on. The Sibuna members let out cheers of relief and victory.

One by one they crossed the beam until they were all safely on the other side. Taking a deep breath, Nina consulted the map and forged on, with the other Sibuna members following behind. They walked through a winding tunnel and rounded a corner. Their faces fell.

The tunnel stopped at a blank stone wall. It was a dead end.

"I'm too tired to try to solve this," said Nina. "Let's call it a night, guys."

Later, Nina was fast asleep in her bed. As she lay motionless, a ghostly light filled the room. Awakened by the glow, Nina opened her eyes. The malevolent spirit she had seen in the attic was staring right at her.

"You sleep soundly, girl. Your stone impasse does not trouble you?" the spirit sneered.

"I've got four other people trying to figure this out with me," Nina protested.

The spirit glowered. "Yes. Your servants. Lazy, fearful creatures. Perhaps if they too shared the mark . . ."

Nina bolted upright. "Shared?"

The spirit showed her palms, and the Anubis signs began to glow. "I will bind them to you," she declared.

"No!" cried Nina.

Behind the spirit, Amber sat up in bed. She screamed, clutching her ankle. In a flash, the spirit disappeared.

Nina rushed over to Amber's bed. "Amber!"

Amber rolled her sock down. Nina looked at Amber's leg with horror: Amber had been branded with the jackal mark too.

"I'm cursed, aren't I?" Amber moaned.

Nina's face showed only shock and terror.

The next morning, Nina and Amber were getting ready for school. "I'm so sorry, Amber. I didn't want this for you. I just . . . I feel so powerless against this thing," Nina told her best friend sadly.

"It's okay. Hey, I was with you anyway. Now I'm just . . . *really* with you," Amber replied as Patricia burst through the door. She thrust her wrist out to them, showing her jackal mark.

"What do you call this?" she demanded.

Amber showed Patricia the mark on her leg. "Membership?"

Just then, Alfie rushed into Nina and Amber's room. "I'm freaking out! I just acquired a tattoo overnight!" He lifted his pajama leg to show the mark of Anubis. "I'm too young, it's illegal, and if I'd had a choice, I would've gone for some sort of fire-breathing dragon!"

Patricia turned to Nina. "Does this mean we're cursed? Are our lives at risk too?"

Nina stared at her, summoning courage, and finally nodded. "I'm sorry, guys," she said, on the verge of tears.

"Hey, it's okay. We just need to solve this mystery, pronto," said Amber.

That night, the Sibuna members searched every inch of the dead end.

"There's nothing here," groaned Patricia.

"Keep looking," said Nina.

Fabian stopped and sighed. "Patricia's right. We've been at this forever. We have to face facts. There's nothing here."

"Why don't we just break through it? Just run at it and smash it with our shoulders," suggested Alfie.

Amber furrowed her eyebrows. "With *your* shoulders?"

Alfie frowned. He took a determined breath and

ran at the wall. With a yell, he hit the wall at full force—and bounced off it, hurtling into Fabian, who stumbled into a side wall. The two went down with a crash.

Fabian jumped up and turned around. The part of the wall he'd hit had opened inward! The Sibuna members crowded around the wall, where they found a small hatch. Dust and soot had hidden the edges, making it invisible before.

Fabian examined the hatch and then opened it. Beyond the hatch was a crawl space only a few feet wide and high. It was dark, dirty, cobwebbed, and full of bugs.

"So who's going into that creepy tunnel of doom first?" Nina asked. "Rock, paper, scissors?"

The Sibuna members exchanged an anxious look, then slowly lifted their fists to play.

Nina shone her flashlight to illuminate the creepy crawl space. She gulped. "I was never good at rock, paper, scissors," she moaned.

Fabian crouched next to Nina. "You'll be fine. Just . . . be careful."

"I'll try. Let's get this over with." Nina crawled in. After a few feet, the tunnel started to narrow. It grew tighter and tighter. Suddenly, Nina's flashlight went out. Nina struggled to stay calm as she breathed in the utter blackness. It was getting difficult to move. Tears welled in her eyes. She was scared.

She banged the flashlight hard against the ground, frantically trying to make it work again. The flashlight flared to life, illuminating a skull directly in front of her! Nina covered her mouth in horror as insects crawled over it.

Desperately trying not to scream, Nina studied the skull. With a jolt, she realized there was a recess in the stone wall behind it.

Steeling herself, Nina reached past the skull and into the recess. Her fingers closed on a lever there and she pulled it hard. She heard a clunking noise from behind the wall.

"Open sesame—I hope," she whispered.

When Nina emerged from the tunnel, the Sibuna members cheered. Amber helped Nina to her feet and hugged her. "Did it work?" asked Nina. She turned and yelped happily. A door had opened in the blank stone wall! "Okay, let's see what Frobisher-Smythe has in store for us next!"

The Sibuna members exchanged grins and walked through the doorway, which led down a series of steps into another tunnel.

At the end of the tunnel the students stopped, stunned.

Ahead of them lay a large room shaped like an octagon. There were drawings of spiders everywhere. Blocking their path was a weblike lattice of threads that crisscrossed the entire room.

"This just keeps getting weirder," said Amber.

Nina caught a glimpse of the big recessed outline of a spider on the far wall. "Look at that spider. It looks like an indentation. Do you think something goes in there?"

"I'm hoping not a giant spider," groaned Amber.

"Look at these threads," said Fabian. The threads were different colors—silver, yellow, and red. Fabian leaned closer and saw a gloopy substance on the threads. He frowned. "Weird."

"Hey, look!" Nina spotted a door on the other side of the tunnel. "That's where we have to get to."

Nina is thrilled to be back for her second year at
Anubis House . . . until a vengeful ghost named
Senkhara puts her and her friends in danger.

Can Fabian keep Nina safe from the wrath of Senkhara,
or will he lose everything trying to save her?

Joy and Fabian used to be best friends, but now Joy wants something more. How far will she go to break up Nina and Fabian?

When bad boy Eddie arrives at Anubis House,
sparks fly between him and Patricia.

Amber and Alfie—the beauty queen and the king of pranks—make a zany and entertaining couple.

When Mara's boyfriend, Mick, moves to Australia, Mara finds herself
drawn to Jerome. Who will she choose—the jock or the jokester?

It's another year of crushes and curses for the guys in Anubis House.

When it comes to adventure and romance,
the Anubis House girls are ready!

"So let's go, then!" said Alfie. He surged forward, touching a bright silver thread. He yelped in pain as a bright red mark appeared on his hand.

"I think there's some kind of venom on all the threads," said Fabian. He peered farther into the room. "And what are those?"

The Sibuna members stared at the three hooks hanging from the ceiling—one yellow, one silver, and one red.

"Let's not worry about it now," said Nina, glancing worriedly at Alfie's hand. "We'll come back tomorrow."

10

Over the next few days, the Sibuna members tried everything to solve the giant spiderweb puzzle. They recreated the thread maze using yarn from the art department and practiced slipping through it. They studied spiders in ancient Egypt but came up with nothing useful. And they still had no idea what the hooks on the ceiling were for, or why there was a huge spider-shaped indentation on the wall.

One afternoon, Nina sat on her bed, clutching her amulet. "Come on, Sarah. A little help now would be great!" Just as she spoke, a tiny bright light filled a room in Sarah's dollhouse. Nina rushed over to the dollhouse and opened it. She moved in for a closer look and noticed that a corner of the wallpaper was peeling off the wall of the tiny dining room.

Nina pinched the corner with her thumb and forefinger and pulled on it slowly. The paper came away completely, and she turned it over in her hand to reveal a riddle on the back. Nina read aloud, "'Upon the foundation on which this house rests, lies the solution to the spiderweb test. To find the armorer and scholar's hollow, the silver thread of fate you must follow.'" Nina smiled. "Thank you, Sarah," she whispered.

Nina turned to the door to share the riddle with her friends—and almost jumped out of her skin. The spirit was standing before her. The specter stepped toward Nina menacingly. "This ruler may be forgotten, but she will not be ignored. Or you will pay the gravest price of all." Her voice filled the room. "You belong to me now, Chosen One, and I will not tolerate any more failure. And do not forget—watch the timepiece." With a cackle, she disappeared.

Later that day, the Sibuna members gathered in the living room. Fabian studied the riddle as Nina filled everyone in on the ghost's threat. "She said,

'This ruler may be forgotten, but she will not be ignored.'" Nina shuddered.

"That sounds like a spirit with self-esteem issues," said Alfie, chuckling.

"So, what's the latest with the clue, Fabian?" asked Amber.

Fabian held up the riddle. "It's pretty obscure." He read it aloud. "'Upon the foundation on which this house rests, lies the solution to the spiderweb test. To find the armorer and scholar's hollow, the silver thread of fate you must follow.'"

Nina frowned. "What's an 'armorer and scholar's hollow'?"

They all thought for a long moment.

"Isn't 'scholar' like an old-style word for a massive nerd?" asked Alfie.

"And where do you find nerds?" asked Amber. She looked pointedly at Fabian.

"The library!" crowed Alfie.

They all looked at Fabian, who bristled. "So I spend a lot of time in the library. That doesn't mean I'm a massive nerd, okay?"

Nina came to Fabian's rescue. "Fabian and I will

research online, while Amber, Patricia, and Alfie can go check out the library. Sound good?"

"Sibuna!" chimed the students.

That night, the Sibuna members gathered in Nina and Amber's room. "So, any luck?" asked Nina.

Alfie shook his head. "We checked the library. No 'armorer' or 'hollows' or 'silver threads of fate.' Just your normal nerd-herd of dorks with books."

Fabian looked up from a book he had been reading. "Wait, I think I've found something." He held the book in the air. "This is all about last names and what they mean. So I thought I'd look up 'Frobisher,' which comes from an old French word, *fourbisseor,* which means 'to shine.'"

Amber rolled her eyes. "Fascinating. And he says he's not a nerd."

Fabian ignored Amber. "Fourbisseor was a last name most commonly given to armorers."

"So the riddle is about the Frobisher-Smythes!" said Nina excitedly.

"Well, he was a scholar, wasn't he?" Alfie pointed out.

Fabian grinned. "Yeah. And 'foundations' could mean founders. And who built this place?"

"The Frobisher-Smythes!" exclaimed Nina. "The picture of them in the dining room—maybe the solution to the task is behind it!"

That night, the Sibuna gang stood in the dining room before a large portrait of the Frobisher-Smythes. Nina lifted it gently off the wall to reveal a bright, unfaded square where the picture had hung. Fabian tapped the wall, starting with the area outside the square, and then inside the square. "It's definitely hollow," he said, tapping the inside again.

"I wonder what this does," mused Alfie. He had found a length of very thin wire hidden behind the picture.

"The 'silver thread of fate'!" gasped Nina.

Alfie took hold of the wire and pulled it. There was a faint sound of cogs clanking and grinding into action behind the wall. The sounds grew louder. A sudden and very loud *clank* came from above, and a large, dark shape dropped from the ceiling behind them. Amber shrieked as the gang turned to face a metallic spider dangling from a wire.

Nina reached out and gingerly touched the spider. "I think this is what we've been looking for! It's the spider that fits in the hole in the web room."

Fabian tugged the wire, freeing the spider. He turned it over to reveal writing on the underside. "'To pass beyond the weaver's throne, lay her daughters in their home. Move with care through her poisoned loom, the scarlet thread may spell your doom,'" he read aloud.

Patricia poked the spider. "Spiders weave webs. So her 'throne' must be the big web in the tunnel!"

"But who are her daughters, and where are they?" asked Amber.

The next day, Nina and Amber were quietly studying on the bed when suddenly the door was thrown open and Alfie barged in, screaming and clawing at the large metallic spider on his back. "It's alive! It's eating me!"

Amber screamed and jumped to her feet. Then

she realized the spider wasn't real. "Alfie!" She rolled up one of her magazines and attacked Alfie with it, knocking the spider to the floor.

Alfie put his hands up, laughing. "Amber, relax, it was just a joke!"

"Hilarious," fumed Amber. She looked at the spider. "And now you've broken it!" The back of the large spider had popped open, and three smaller spiders had fallen out. "Ew, they're all gross and tiny, like spider babies."

Nina leapt to her feet. "Guys—the riddle said 'lay her daughters in their home.' Well, if the big spider is the mom, then could these three little spiders be her daughters?" She grinned broadly. "There are three spiders, and three hooks on the web. I think we've solved our riddle!"

That evening, before the Sibuna gang headed to the spiderweb, Nina and Fabian were in the Frobisher Library helping Jasper organize the Treasures of Egypt exhibition pieces. Fabian decided to ask Jasper about a "forgotten ruler," to try to gain some insight into the malevolent spirit that was haunting Nina. "Jasper, do you know anything about a 'forgotten' Egyptian ruler?"

Jasper frowned. "Ah, yes. The forgotten ruler. A terrible tyrannical queen. Archeologists found a crown inside an empty tomb. There was no body, nothing."

Meanwhile, Nina was walking along the mezzanine toward a display shelf. On it was an ancient crown. Nina gasped. She recognized the scarab-and-twin-snake design carved into it. She reached out slowly and touched the crown. The voice of the wrathful spirit filled her head.

"Senkhara," Nina whispered, her voice filled with horror.

"Yes, that's her name. How did you know?" Jasper said, looking at Nina in amazement.

11

It was well past midnight when the Sibuna gang reached the giant spiderweb. Moving slowly, Patricia, Nina, and Fabian worked their way carefully around the threads to the hanging hooks. Fabian had attached the large spider to his back, and each student carried a metal baby spider. One by one, they hung the spiders on the hooks.

As Fabian hung the last baby spider on its hook, they all heard the sound of grinding stone, and the door at the far end of the room opened! Amber and Patricia cheered.

But as soon as the door was fully open, it slowly started to close again. Determined not to lose her chance to find out what was behind the next door, Nina hurriedly picked her way through the final threads. The door was barely open when she finally reached it.

"No, Nina, don't!" cried Fabian.

Nina looked behind her. "This might be the only chance I get!" She slipped through the entrance just as the door thudded shut.

There was silence. Then the Sibuna members heard Nina scream. "I think there's something in here!" she cried. "Help! You have to get me out!"

"I'm coming, Nina!" called Fabian. He raced through the web, dodging and ducking the terrible threads until he came to the spider-shaped recess by the door. He ripped the spider off his back and slammed it into the recess.

Nothing happened.

"Help me!" wailed Nina.

Fabian banged his fist against the wall in frustration. As he did, they heard the distant clanking and whirring of machinery. And, as fast as lightning, the threads retracted into the walls.

The door slowly started to open, and this time it didn't close. Nina rushed out and into Fabian's arms. She had never been so terrified in her life, and as she hugged Fabian, she realized how much he meant to her.

"Thanks for saving me, Fabian," she said tearfully.

Fabian held her for a long moment before reluctantly letting her go. He didn't say anything, but Nina felt her heart flutter as he gazed at her. Wiping away her tears, she smiled bravely. "Come on, guys, let's see what's behind door number three!"

The Sibuna gang followed a tunnel that led beyond the spiderweb room and entered the next chamber. They saw a strange-looking checkerboard on the floor, four squares wide and ten squares long, marked with Egyptian symbols. Four imposing jackal-headed guard statues had been strategically placed upon the board, each one holding a spear and a shield. But there was no mask. In front of the board was a tall, thronelike stone chair.

"Whoa," said Alfie. He moved to cross the board. Instinctively, Fabian and Nina pulled him back.

"Wait, Alfie!" said Nina. "We don't want to rush in. It might be a trap."

Fabian looked down at the squares, his eyebrows furrowed in concentration. "I think this is an ancient Egyptian game. I've seen this board before, but I'll need to look it up. Come on, let's go. We can figure this out tomorrow. We've had more than enough excitement for one night."

But the next day while the students were eating lunch, Vera appeared and asked Nina to step into the hallway. When they were out of earshot of the others, Vera gently told Nina, "The hospital called just after you left for school. I'm afraid your gran has taken ill. And the doctors would like you to go to the hospital straightaway."

Nina reeled in shock. Numbly, she thanked Vera and went to tell the Sibuna gang. Fabian offered to go to the hospital with her, and Nina gratefully accepted.

At the hospital, the doctors told Nina that her grandmother had suddenly and inexplicably fallen into a coma. After telling Fabian that she wanted some time alone with her grandmother, Nina took a deep breath and entered the hospital room. She found Gran in bed, unconscious and hooked up to machines. As she held her grandmother's hand, Nina couldn't stop the tears from rolling down her cheeks.

A few minutes passed before Fabian came hesitantly through the door. When he saw the expression on Nina's face, he immediately went to her and gave her a long hug. "What did the doctors say?" he asked.

Nina wiped her tears with her sleeve. "They're very concerned." Her voice broke. "I just don't understand."

Fabian moved to the foot of Gran's bed. He picked up the doctor's notes and studied them. "It looks like the doctors are as confused as we are." He read further. "'Evelyn Meridian Martin.' That's an unusual middle name—Meridian."

Nina sniffled. "It's some sort of family name."

Fabian frowned. He rustled the notes. "It says she took ill in London."

Nina nodded. "At some tourist attraction. The Royal Observatory in Greenwich."

Fabian muttered, "Greenwich . . . Greenwich." His eyes widened. "You know what else is in Greenwich?" Nina stared at him blankly. "The International Meridian!"

Nina shook her head, uncomprehending. "Okay. So?"

"Greenwich Mean Time. GMT! Your gran got ill

right on top of the International Meridian. For time. I think your gran might be—"

Nina gasped, finally understanding. "You think Gran is the timepiece that Senkhara keeps warning me about?" With a knot of dread in her stomach, she pulled up the sleeve of Gran's nightgown.

There, just above her grandmother's elbow—was the Mark of Anubis.

12

After her visit to the hospital, Nina arrived back at Anubis House completely exhausted. She went to her room and collapsed into her bed. Shortly afterward, Amber arrived, followed by Patricia. Even though all she wanted was to put her head into her pillow and cry, Nina summoned the strength to fill in her friends about her grandmother's illness.

When she was done, Amber patted her hand sympathetically. "I can't believe it," she said.

Patricia shook her head in disbelief. "You mean the timepiece is Granny Martin?"

Nina nodded. "She's been hexed, just like us."

Amber pulled Nina into a big hug. "Senkhara's one mean spirit lady."

"I know." Nina squared her shoulders. "We need to figure out the next task in the tunnels fast—I'm not going to lose you guys, or Gran, to Senkhara!"

During study period the next day, Fabian summoned the other Sibuna members to look at his laptop, where he had been researching. He showed the gang what he had found. "I searched for ancient Egyptian games, and this is what came up." He clicked on some pictures.

Nina peered at the screen. "'Senet,'" she read.

Amber nodded, looking at the picture. "That's our board!"

Fabian shook his head. "Well, similar." He pointed to one section of the screen. "It says here that no one knows the exact rules as played by the ancient Egyptians."

"It's a start," declared Nina. "Print it off. We'll bring the picture of the Senet board down tonight and compare it with the board in the tunnels."

Later that night, Nina, Fabian, Amber, Patricia, and Alfie crept through the tunnels until they were standing before the checkered floor. When they arrived, they compared the picture of the Senet board from the Internet with the real board in the tunnel.

After a few minutes Fabian announced, "It's basically the same game, except without the playing pieces."

Nina pointed to the stone figures on the board. "And the guards. What are they all about?"

Alfie groaned. "Let's face it—we have no idea what we're doing. We might as well get this over with." To the horror of the others, Alfie took a step onto the board.

"Alfie! No!" cried Nina.

Just then, the students heard a deep grinding noise underneath the floor. Alfie glanced nervously around. "What's happening?" he called.

Slowly, a panel at the far end of the board lifted, revealing a glass cabinet. A golden light played across the faces of the amazed Sibuna gang. Nina's eyes grew wider than ever. "The Mask of Anubis!" she whispered.

A gleaming mask in the shape of a jackal's face rested inside the cabinet. It was flawlessly crafted, with perfect eyeholes and a smooth, elongated nose.

There was a small third hole directly in the center of the mask's forehead. The four imposing Anubis statues stood on squares to the left and right of it.

Wordlessly, the Sibuna members gazed at the mask. Finally, Amber spoke. "It's sooo pretty. For a dog mask."

"What are we waiting for?" cried Alfie. He took another step forward on the board, and then froze as a fifth Anubis statue appeared through the floor. It was more armed than the others, holding both a spear and a sword. As it rose, it obscured the students' view of the mask.

Alfie jumped back with a yelp. At that moment, the crackly voice of Robert Frobisher-Smythe filled the room. *The golden prize will tempt the fool. The wise should heed this golden rule. This game of Senet you cannot win. Only the reckless will even begin. One wrong move will seal your fate. An end too dark to contemplate.*

The recording ended.

Alfie gulped and moved off the board to rejoin the Sibuna gang, breathing a sigh of relief. "Okay, what does that mean?" he asked.

"It means we need to be absolutely sure of the rules before we even think about playing," replied Fabian gravely.

Patricia raised her eyebrows. "We're thinking of playing?"

Nina nodded. "Patricia's right," she told the gang. "It's too dangerous. This one I do on my own."

"No!" Fabian stepped in front of Nina. "What if we need other players? Nina, I will not let you do this by yourself." He turned to look at the others. "We all got the mark, not just Nina. We can do this."

13

The next evening in the Frobisher Library, Nina, Fabian, Amber, Patricia, and Alfie gathered around a small table, excited by a new discovery. After noticing that the library floor was tiled exactly like a Senet board, Amber had found a mismatched tile. When the Sibuna members pried it up, it turned out to be Robert Frobisher-Smythe's Senet board—complete with playing instructions! Now they were trying to figure out the rules of the game.

Patricia pointed to the board. "So it's a cross between Snakes and Ladders and checkers?"

Alfie grinned. "Check-n-Chadders! Checkadders! No, no, no. Sneckers!"

Fabian groaned. "Look, the journey across the board represents the journey from this life to the afterlife."

Nina peered at the directions. "The rules look kind of lopsided."

Patricia nodded. "Like pawns versus queens."

Fabian spoke up. "Or humans versus gods."

The Sibuna gang puzzled over the rules for hours, but it still looked to be an unfair game with very little chance for them to win. When the clock struck nine, they decided to call it a night. They all headed back to Anubis House before their ten o'clock curfew.

The next evening, Nina went to the hospital. As she sat holding her grandmother's hand, she tried to encourage her to wake up. "You haven't even been to Scotland, Gran, so you can't quit your tour just yet! You've got to get better." Nina's voice broke. "You've just got to!"

Gran's eyes flew open. Nina gasped. But her grandmother's eyes were utterly black. "Nina," Gran growled.

Nina screamed when she recognized Senkhara's wrathful gaze and icy voice.

"Foolish girl. Such a disappointment," Senkhara sneered.

"What have you done to my gran?" cried Nina.

Suddenly, Nina's grandmother's face softened, and her voice returned to normal. "Nina, help me. You must do as she asks." Then her face hardened into Senkhara's again. "You heard what she said. Now, bring me the mask!" commanded the evil spirit.

"I will!" sobbed Nina. "Just don't hurt her!"

Nina lifted her head with a jerk. She realized she had fallen asleep by Gran's bedside. She looked at her beloved grandmother's peaceful, sleeping face. Nina rested her head wearily on Gran's hand and held it tightly in her own.

When Nina arrived back at Anubis House, everyone had gone to bed except the Sibuna members. Over a cold dinner, Nina told them what had happened at the hospital.

Alfie shivered. "Senkhara spoke through your gran? That is seriously scary."

Nina nodded. "Believe me, it was. We have to get her that mask!"

"We will," declared Fabian, giving Nina a determined look.

Amber sighed. "Thing is, has anyone wondered what Senkhara's going to do with it? I mean, she can hardly wear it as an accessory. She's a ghost."

Fabian rolled his eyes. "I don't think Senkhara's really interested in fashion, Amber."

Nina stood up. "Who cares what she wants it for? She's asked for the mask and we're going to give it to her, so we can be free of this."

The next day, Nina, Fabian, Amber, and Alfie gathered in Nina and Amber's room to practice playing Senet. After a few moves, Fabian muttered, "I think I'm getting the hang of it. You just have to get past the gods without landing on a danger square." He pointed to the squares surrounding the statues with the Mark of Anubis on them. "If you land on one of those, you lose your life."

Nina shuddered. "Metaphorically speaking—I hope."

Just then, Patricia entered. "Hey, guys, how's it going so far?"

"Fabian's managed to get past the guards two times out of four," said Alfie.

"Greeeaat," said Patricia sarcastically. "So we have a fifty-fifty chance of suffering an 'end too dark to contemplate.'"

Fabian gritted his teeth. "Or a fifty-fifty chance of getting across the board and to the mask." He went back to practicing.

As she watched him play, Nina came to a decision. "We have to go down tonight," she declared.

Amber's eyes widened. "No! We're not ready."

Fabian grimaced. "We're as ready as we'll ever be."

Nina nodded. "And we're running out of time, Amber." She looked at the Sibuna members. "For Gran. For me. Maybe for all of us."

14

It was past midnight. While most students lay fast asleep, five teenagers crept through the tunnels under Anubis House until they entered the room with the Senet board. Trembling, Fabian climbed onto the stone chair. From where he sat, he could see the entire board. "Let the game begin," he said hoarsely.

Nina, Amber, Patricia, and Alfie lined up nervously alongside the board.

"Here's how it works," said Fabian. He pointed to the armed Anubis statues. "Those guards are our opponents. First we make our move. Then it's their turn."

Alfie gulped nervously. "And how do they move, exactly?"

Fabian shrugged. "We don't know yet. All I know is I need to get one of you safely to the other side of the board. And remember—an Anubis piece can only take you if you're on a danger square. Those are the ones with a jackal mark." He pointed to the squares on the board clustered around the Anubis guards.

Nina shuddered. "Well, what happens if we're taken?"

"Let's hope we never find out," said Fabian grimly.

"*So* not reassured," drawled Patricia.

Fabian took a deep breath. "Okay. Our side moves four squares each time—so that's one square each. Amber. Go forward one square."

Amber squealed. "Me? Alfie said he really wanted to go first."

"I never cut in front of a lady," Alfie said quickly.

"Amber. Do it," commanded Fabian.

Tentatively, Amber did as she was told.

"Okay, Nina and Patricia, move forward one square. Alfie, you too." Fabian nodded encouragingly.

Patricia moved forward one square. Then Nina did. Finally, Alfie stepped, trembling, onto the board.

The sounds of cogs and wheels grinding filled the room. All five Anubis statues revolved. The statues each held a spear, and each statue pointed its spear at a different empty square.

The Sibuna members laughed with relief.

"Is that all you've got, Frobisher-Smythe?" chortled Alfie. "This is going to be a piece of cake."

Fabian led the Sibuna gang carefully around the board, gaining a little more ground with each move. Finally, Nina and Amber approached one of the Anubis guards.

"Amber, one square forward," called Fabian.

Amber looked down. The square in front of her bore the jackal mark. "But that's a danger square. How come everyone else gets a safe one?"

Fabian groaned. "Look, I don't have any choice, Amber. Please. Just do it."

Amber closed her eyes and stepped forward. Stone ground on stone as all the statues on the board began to rotate.

Amber screamed and ducked as an Anubis statue's spear arced over her square. The spear passed her and pointed to another square.

"Good job, Fabian! What now?" asked Nina.

Fabian bit his lip in concentration. "Nina, Patricia, and Alfie—forward one square. Amber, one square to your left. I know it's a danger square. I'm sorry."

"I really hate this game," moaned Amber.

Nina smiled tightly at her. "It's okay, I'll be on a danger square too."

"Look, if I'm right, you'll both be safe," said Fabian.

"Don't worry Fabian, I trust you," said Nina, stepping forward.

Once everyone moved, the statues revolved. Amber ducked again as a spear passed over her. Nina ducked too as the statue next to her swung its spear across her square—and passed her. Nina let out the breath she had been holding.

But then the statue quickly swung back and pointed straight at Nina. The square she was standing on opened. With a scream, Nina disappeared into the ground.

"Nina!" cried Fabian.

15

Nina blacked out as she fell for what seemed like forever. When she slowly came around, she was in a stone cell about eight feet wide and ten feet across. There was no furniture except two wooden crates. Weak light filtered through a small rectangular opening at the top of one of the walls. There were iron bars across the opening.

Nina stood up and shakily placed her hands against the walls, fruitlessly searching for a way out. "Hello? Can anyone hear me!" she yelled.

A deep, gloomy voice filled the room. "I assure you. There is no way out."

Nina turned to see Victor standing in front of her. "Victor! What are you doing here?" She shook her head. "It doesn't matter. Get me out!" she cried.

Victor spoke. "Impossible! As I found at great cost to myself. Many, many years ago."

Nina stared at him. She suddenly realized he was wearing nineteenth-century clothing, sported an antique gold ring, carried a walking cane—and was transparent. She paled. "You're not Victor," she gasped.

The apparition banged its cane. "My name is Victor Rodenmaar Senior. I assume you are referring to my worthless son?"

Nina backed away, terrified. "But if you're Victor Senior, then you must be . . ."

"Dead as a dodo, my dear. Yes," said the ghost.

"Then that means I'm—" Nina felt the world spinning around her.

The ghost shook its head. "Quite the contrary. You are very much alive."

But it was talking to no one. Nina had fainted.

When Nina awoke again, she had no idea how much time had passed. All she knew was that she was trapped in a dungeon and would most likely die there, with only the ghost of Victor's father to keep her company. She was tired and hungry, and on the verge of breaking down.

As she leaned her head against the wall, she heard voices trickling down from the opening above. One of them sounded like Fabian's! It had to be her imagination, but Nina decided to call for help anyway. "Hello? I'm down here, can you hear me?" she yelled.

"It's Nina!" she heard Fabian exclaim. "Nina! Where are you?"

"I'm here, I'm down here!" Nina called. "Where are you?"

"Amber and I are in Mr. Sweet's office. Hang on, Nina, we'll get you out of there!"

"Fabian, Mr. Sweet's coming!" cried Amber.

"Nina, we've got to go, but we'll come back for you soon!" Fabian's promise rolled down into the cell, and Nina wept with relief. She heard Mr. Sweet talking to her friends, and then . . . silence.

Nina waited, but her friends didn't come back. As she paced the cell, the air rippled, and the ghost of Victor Senior appeared. Nina rubbed her eyes. "I thought I'd dreamed you," she said.

The spirit shrugged. "Some people have the gift to see and others not. Your gift is great."

"Yeah, so great I ended up getting benched." Nina looked at the ghost. "So. How did you end up down here?"

The ghost's face grew sad. "I sought the power of the mask, but Robert was too clever for me. And my own son was too stupid to find me. Nobody came. I was left here to rot."

Nina shivered. "My friends are going to get me out."

The spirit regarded her pityingly. "For your sake, I hope they do." It started to fade.

"No, wait!" cried Nina. "What did you mean about the power of the mask?"

But the spirit was gone.

Nina sat on the floor of the cell, her knees drawn up under her. She was cold, hungry, and feeling very alone. She rocked back and forth, on the verge of tears. It had been a long time since she had heard Fabian's voice.

Suddenly, she heard the faint sound of someone calling her name. She jumped to her feet. "I'm down here!" she hollered.

Amber's voice floated into the cell. "Fabian and I are going to throw you down some supplies." A bottle of water and a bag of food tumbled down the vent. Nina stretched her fingers through the bars of the window and grabbed them. "Thank you!" she said, gulping down the water and tearing open the bag.

"Nina, just hang in there. We'll get you out really, really soon," said Fabian.

"Totally!" chimed in Amber. Then Nina heard her say in a lowered voice, "Good call, Fabian—we don't want her to know we're totally stumped."

Nina's blood ran cold. As she heard her friends leave, she looked despairingly at the plastic bag. She wasn't hungry anymore.

"Eat. Drink. You must keep your strength up if you are to survive."

Nina jumped and looked up. Victor Senior was

standing before her. "I thought you'd left me to rot," she said.

The ghost shook its head. "Not a nice feeling, rotting. You, at least, have people who care about you. When I disappeared, no one came."

Nina's eyes widened. "Not even your son?"

The ghost's eyes grew spiteful. "Especially not my son." After a moment, the ghost sighed. "I have come to realize I'd brought it all upon myself, Chosen One."

Nina paused. "What does it mean exactly? To be the Chosen One?"

"You don't know? You are a direct descendent of the high priestess Amneris. You are Chosen. The paragon!"

"The . . . paragon?" Nina couldn't believe what she was hearing.

The ghost continued. "And the Osirian is your protector. Together you keep the world safe."

Nina gasped. "What? Wait, wait, wait. Rewind. The world?"

"You cannot escape your destiny," the spirit proclaimed solemnly. "Like sun and moon. Like yin and yang. The Chosen One has always had her counterpart. The paragon and the Osirian have been paired together throughout the centuries to keep the world safe."

Nina stumbled back, stunned. "So who's my yang?"

"You do not know," replied Victor Senior. "But one thing is certain. He will not be far away."

16

Hours passed. To keep her mind distracted, Nina recited the U.S. states in alphabetical order. She had gotten up to Iowa when a trapdoor appeared in the ceiling and Alfie tumbled into the cell! Nina rushed to him, but he was out cold. A short time later, Fabian's voice came down the vent. "Nina, can you hear me?"

Nina jumped to her feet and shouted back. "Yes! Yes, I can hear you!"

"Is Alfie with you?"

Nina looked at Alfie, who was starting to wake up. "Yeah, he's here. A little shaken up, but he's good."

"Nina, I'm sending down his favorite snacks," said Amber. "Look after him for me, won't you?" Chocolate bars sailed down, followed by two cans of soda. Alfie groggily made a grab for one of the chocolate bars.

"We tried the game again. Alfie got caught by one of the guards on a danger square. Please tell Alfie I'm sorry. It was a stupid idea." Fabian's voice was filled with regret.

Alfie called out shakily, "Hey! It could have worked. You had to try."

"We're going to get you both out of there soon, all right? Next time we play, we'll figure it out. I promise." Fabian sounded determined.

In the cell that night, Alfie quickly went to sleep, but Nina couldn't shut her eyes. As she huddled in the corner, Victor Senior appeared. He looked at the sleeping Alfie. "Another seeker of the mask?"

Nina nodded. "Yes. He's on my side." She paused. "You said the mask had special powers. What does it do? And why were you searching for it?"

Victor Senior sighed. "I wanted the tears of gold, of course. I longed for immortality in the life I knew, not some Egyptian afterlife."

Nina was confused. "Egyptian afterlife?"

"Yes. Whoever wears the Mask of Anubis will become as a god. But the tears of gold that the mask weeps are key to the Elixir of Life, to keep one alive forever in your world." The spirit bowed its head. "But I failed. And I shall shortly be taking my leave from you. For many years I have waited for someone like you to come, so that I may finally pass on my message."

"A message to whom?" asked Nina.

"To my worthless son. Tell him—" The spirit hesitated. It suddenly looked very old and very sad. "Tell him I am sorry. And that I was the worthless one after all."

The spirit started to disappear. As it left, Nina spotted something glinting on the floor. It was Victor Senior's gold ring.

"Give it to my son," said the spirit's voice. "Beware Senkhara; she means you harm. Farewell, Chosen One."

And with that, the voice faded away.

The next day brought two more surprises. Nina was pacing up and down the cell when Amber and Patricia fell into the dungeon, two more victims of the Senet board. As soon as Amber saw Alfie, she scrambled to her feet and flew into his arms. "Alfie! I missed you!"

"I missed you too, Ambs," replied Alfie, surprised. As Amber hugged him tighter, he gasped, "Okay, you have to let go now."

Amber gave Alfie one last squeeze before giving Nina a big hug too. "And you, Neens." Amber's nose wrinkled. "Oh, wow. I say this with love, but you really need a shower."

Nina laughed. "There is nothing I'd like more."

A short while later, Amber, Patricia, Alfie, and Nina sat on the floor, eating some of the provisions. Amber broke a chocolate bar into squares and handed them out. "I'm glad one of us came prepared," she said.

As they ate, Patricia stared glumly at her chocolate square. "Let's just face it, we are never going to get out of here," she moaned.

Just then, they detected the muffled voices of Joy and Fabian on the other side of a wall. Before they could react, they heard the sound of a key being put in a lock. A door materialized out of the solid rock, opening to reveal Fabian and Joy. Nina rushed into Fabian's arms. "I knew you'd do it!" she said tearfully.

Fabian blushed. "I wouldn't have done it if it wasn't for Joy. After I lost all of you to the Senet board I asked her to help. She's a chess champion. She solved the Senet game. She was amazing."

Nina turned to Joy. "Thanks, Joy. I owe you one." Then she realized something. "Wait, the mask. We need to get it!"

Fabian grabbed her arm, stopping her. "Nina, it's still locked away." He held up the key he had used to open the dungeon door. "We had a choice—release you, or release the mask."

17

When she returned to Anubis House, the first thing Nina did was take a long shower. Afterward, she went to her room to change. She was looking in the mirror to adjust her Eye of Horus locket when the back of her neck began to prickle. Nina looked around.

Senkhara was across the room, staring at her with utter hatred. "So, the Chosen One has returned. But without the mask," she spat.

Nina trembled. "We'll get it. I promise."

"Your friends had the key and they discarded it!"

"In order to rescue me!" protested Nina.

Senkhara spoke, her voice bitter and angry. "My patience has run dry with you. The old one will die first. At sundown tomorrow."

Nina paled. "Gran? No, no, please!"

The vengeful spirit continued. "And then who will be next? The pretty girl? Or the clown? The angry girl? Or your precious boy?" It laughed maliciously.

Nina gasped. "If you hurt him—or any of them—"

Senkhara smiled. "At sundown tomorrow, you will know all. And then I will keep my promise and claim your lives." The air rippled—and the spirit disappeared.

That evening, Nina called an emergency Sibuna meeting in her room. As the other members gathered around, she told them about Senkhara's threat. When she was done, Fabian tried to reassure her. "Hey, it's okay. We'll have the mask by tomorrow night. Your gran's going to be fine."

"What else did Senkhara say?" asked Amber.

Nina shuddered. "We have until sundown. And then she's coming after us. One by one."

"Right. Well, perfect. All we need to do is get through a sheet of unbreakable glass!" Alfie's voice was an octave higher than normal. "I mean, why are we even worrying?"

"We need another key to open that glass cabinet," declared Fabian.

Amber rolled her eyes. "Pity Frobisher-Smythe couldn't leave a spare key under the mat like any normal person."

Nina looked thoughtful. "If he did, where would he hide it?" Her eyes brightened. "Remember the doll clue? 'The athenaeum is the place to look. Lift the wings to find the book. Hidden in this book of old: water of life and tears of gold.'" Nina turned to Fabian. "Books can be many things—including the 'key' to solving a mystery. Maybe the 'book' in the doll riddle is a key!"

"That would mean the key is in the library!" Fabian frowned. "We'd better look quickly—Jasper is packing up the ancient Egyptian exhibition today. Now that the exhibition is over, all the artifacts are going back to the museums. If we're not careful, he might pack up the key!"

A few hours later, Nina, Amber, and Joy were in the Frobisher Library, hunting desperately for anything that could give them a clue to the whereabouts of another key. Fabian had stayed behind at Anubis House to do some more research on Senkhara, in hopes of defeating the evil spirit.

Some of the exhibits had already been packed into crates, and the three girls had searched in and around the crates, on the ground floor, everywhere—but had found nothing.

Dispirited, Nina headed to the spiral staircase. As she examined the balustrade, she stopped. At the bottom of the staircase was an etching of two wings!

"'Lift the wings to find the book,'" whispered Nina. Excitedly, she pulled gently on the wings. A secret compartment lined with velvet slid open! But there was nothing inside. Nina felt around the velvet, searching for a clue. Then her fingers touched something hard sewn into the lining.

Nina called Amber over, and Amber pulled a mini manicure kit from her bag. She handed Nina a pair of nail scissors. Holding her breath, Nina cut through the seam in the lining.

Inside was a shiny golden key. Nina picked it up triumphantly. "Yes! Let's go."

The three girls raced through the tunnels until they arrived at the chamber containing the mask.

Nina stopped in shock. The Anubis statues had disappeared! Now there was only the smooth checkered floor leading to the glass cabinet. As they approached the mask, Nina, Joy, and Amber stared warily at it.

"Okay. Fingers crossed. And watch out for booby traps," warned Nina. She took out the key and hesitated, glancing at Amber, who gave her an encouraging look. Bracing herself, Nina put the key in the lock.

The girls each took a deep breath. The key turned, and the glass cabinet opened.

18

Nina carefully removed the mask from its pedestal and held it high. "Senkhara!" she called. "I have the mask. Come and get it!"

Senkhara appeared at the far side of the board. Joy let out an involuntary yelp as the spirit glided across the chamber, looking hungrily at the mask.

"How come we can see Senkhara now?" Amber whispered to Nina.

"Senkhara's getting what she wants," Nina replied. "She doesn't care who sees her now."

Then Senkhara was directly in front of Nina. Her smile was chilling. "Finally. It is mine," she breathed. Her smile disappeared, and she glared at Nina. "Put it on," she commanded.

Nina took a step back. "What?"

Senkhara repeated darkly, "Put it on."

"Don't put it on," Joy said, shuddering.

"Why does she want you to put it on?" howled Amber.

Nina raised the mask toward her face just as Fabian came hurtling into the chamber. He had discovered a terrible secret about the mask. When he couldn't find Nina anywhere else, he had guessed that she was in the mask chamber.

"Nina! Stop!" cried Fabian.

"Do not listen to him!" Senkhara thundered.

Fabian grabbed Nina's arm. "Senkhara needs a real human body to transport her to the afterlife. She can't put on the mask herself because she's a ghost, so she's planning to use you. If you put on that mask, we'll lose you forever!"

"What?" gasped Amber, horrified.

Nina hesitated—and then steeled herself. She turned to the spirit. "Will you lift the curse off Gran and my friends?"

Senkhara nodded. "Yes. Now put on the mask."

Nina put on the mask.

A moment passed.

And then another.

Senkhara's face darkened. "Why is nothing

happening?" she screamed as Nina took the mask from her face. "You are not the paragon. I shall have to seek my champion elsewhere. For you all, it's over!"

The mark on Nina's arm began to glow, and Nina gasped in pain. Fabian and Amber cried out as they felt their marks starting to burn too.

"What is it? What's wrong?" asked Joy anxiously.

As Senkhara started to fade away, Amber shrieked in agony.

"No, Senkhara! Senkhara, wait. Please!" begged Nina. Just then, a flash of light crossed her face. She looked down to see the locket Sarah had given her starting to glow.

Instinctively, Nina held the locket up to the mask. The eyeholes filled with light, beaming two eye-shaped projections onto the wall of the chamber. Writing started to appear in the two projections. As she read the words, Nina called out frantically to the vanishing spirit. "Senkhara! This isn't the true mask! Here's the final clue! The mask *was* meant for me—I am the one you need! Just stop hurting my friends, please!"

Senkhara reappeared, glowering, but her eyes burned with curiosity. "Read," she commanded

Nina. Fabian and Amber gasped with relief as their jackal marks stopped burning.

Nina looked through the mask and read the couplet that was written in the projection of the eyeholes. "'The true mask still awaits, hidden for all to see. The portal of the mind awakes, the paragon is the key.'"

"What does that even mean?" asked Amber.

Joy shook her head, uncomprehending. "How can something be hidden for all to see?"

The Sibuna members thought frantically. Suddenly, Nina had a moment of inspiration. "A museum! The bronze replica! The Frobisher-Smythes donated a replica of the Mask of Anubis to the British Museum, didn't they?"

"That's it!" cried Fabian. "What they donated wasn't a replica—it was the real thing. They hid the Mask of Anubis in plain sight."

"And the replica is sitting in the Frobisher Library as part of the Treasures of Egypt exhibition." Nina put the fake mask back in its chamber and took off toward the tunnels. "To the library, guys!"

"No, Nina!" called Fabian desperately. "Think about what you're doing!"

19

Her heart pounding, Nina ignored Fabian and raced through the tunnels, determined to get to the library. Fabian sprinted after her, leaving Senkhara behind. When she reached the library, Nina went directly to a glass display case where a battered bronze mask lay. Next to the mask was a small placard stating that the object was "a replica of the fabled Mask of Anubis." Trembling, Nina opened the case and took out the mask.

As she held it, gripped by a sense of inevitability, Fabian dashed into the library. "Nina, you don't have to do this!" he cried.

Nina looked at Fabian for a long moment. "I do," she said sadly.

Just then, Amber and Jerome burst in. Unbeknownst to the Sibuna members, Jerome had been solving his own mystery. He had discovered that a gem had been stolen from the Frobisher-Smythes—a gem that turned out to be a missing piece of the Mask of Anubis, its "third eye."

When he had bumped into Amber as she was running toward the library, Jerome had filled Amber in on the history of the Frobisher gem. Together they had raced to get to Nina with their important piece of information.

"Nina! You need the third eye!" exclaimed Amber.

"The Frobisher gem!" huffed Jerome, struggling to catch his breath.

Nina looked from Amber to Jerome to the small indentation on the mask's forehead.

"Do you have the gem, Jerome?" asked Nina.

Jerome shook his head. "I found it, but I don't have it with me right now. I gave it to—"

But before he could finish, the door of the library burst open, and Eddie, the new American student, appeared. He had a glowing amethyst gem in his hand. Patricia was a few steps behind him.

Nina's eyes widened. "Eddie?"

Patricia spoke up, gasping. "He just started

freaking out on me. Mumbling about the Chosen One and the . . . the Osirian? I think he banged his head. . . ."

Nina crossed over to Eddie and stared at him in disbelief. "You're the Osirian?" she whispered. Wordlessly, Eddie nodded.

Nina went to take the gem from Eddie's hand. His fingers closed over it. "Think about what you're doing," he said gravely.

Nina gripped Eddie's wrist and opened his hand. She firmly took the gem from him. Tears formed in her eyes, but she blinked them back.

Fabian ran over and snatched the mask out of Nina's hand. "Please don't do this!" he pleaded.

"I have to, Fabian. It's the only way." Taking a deep breath, Nina carefully placed the Frobisher gem into the hole in the center of the mask.

The mask started to glow. Everyone watched, amazed, as the mask turned from dull bronze to pure gold. As Nina took the mask from Fabian, Senkhara appeared on the library's mezzanine.

Tears streamed from Fabian's eyes as Nina raised the mask to her face.

"Look. Look at the mask," gasped Joy.

The mask had begun to weep golden tears.

The black smoke of Senkhara entered Nina's body, and Senkhara's cruel laugh rang throughout the room. "The Chosen One!" howled Senkhara in triumph as she poured herself into Nina. Then the spirit's voice issued from Nina's mouth. "The field of rushes awaits the Chosen One." Senkhara had taken over Nina's body.

A portal opened on the mezzanine, full of bright white light. Senkhara walked slowly up the stairs toward it.

"No, Nina!" screamed Fabian. He dashed to the bottom of the stairs. Senkhara turned and fired a bolt of black energy at him.

As the energy flashed toward Fabian, Joy threw herself at it. She took the full brunt of the bolt and dropped to the floor. Patricia ran to her side. "Joy! Joy!" Patricia yelled, trying to rouse the stricken girl.

Meanwhile, Eddie was staring at Nina as if in a trance. Suddenly, Amber was beside him. "Don't just stand there. You're the Osirian, whatever that's supposed to mean. Do something!"

Eddie seemed to snap out of it. He looked around

as if he heard voices no one else could hear. "Tell me where," he said. After a moment, he went to one of the packing cases and removed an object from it.

It was Senkhara's crown, glowing in its protective wrapping.

Senkhara, in Nina's body, was now on the mezzanine and about to enter the portal. Before she stepped in, she turned and looked down at Eddie, who held her crown in the air. Senkhara raised a hand and directed one of her black bolts toward him. But with lightning speed, Eddie ducked. In a deep, commanding voice, he shouted, "In the name of Anubis, I banish you. *Neta ankh betta sekhmet. Khala met!*"

"No, Osirian! Nooo!" Senkhara wailed as she separated from Nina's body and became her transparent, ghostly figure once again. The crown disappeared from Eddie's hands.

At that moment, Alfie ran into the library. In his hand he held the fake golden mask from the tunnels. "Rufus and Victor are right behind me!" he yelled. Somehow both Rufus Zeno—who had faked his death and was very much still alive—and Victor had found out about the Mask of Anubis. They had followed the students into the tunnels and were just about to take the fake mask from its chamber when Alfie had gone in and snatched it, running away with the two men in close pursuit.

Rufus ran into the library and spotted Alfie holding the mask from the tunnels. "Give me that, you little—" the vicious man began. Then his eyes were drawn to the mezzanine, where he saw Nina wearing the golden mask, about to step into the open portal. "That's the true mask!" he exclaimed. He bounded up the steps.

"No, no, no! Rufus, stop!" yelled Fabian.

As Victor entered the library, Rufus grabbed the real mask off Nina's face. The tears of gold evaporated, but Nina clung to the mask. She couldn't let Rufus take it, leaving Gran and her friends to Senkhara's curse. So many lives depended on her sacrifice. "Rufus, you mustn't wear it," said Nina tearfully.

Victor called up to Nina. "Let him take it and go!"

"Listen to the old man, child," sneered Rufus.

Victor stared straight into Nina's eyes. "Yes, you listen to this old man," he said.

Something in Victor's tone got through to Nina. She knew he was a cranky house guardian, but she suddenly got the feeling that he genuinely wanted to keep the students safe. Taking a leap of faith, Nina let go of the mask.

With a cry of triumph, Rufus clutched the mask and held it aloft. "Prepare to bow down before me, mortals!" he crowed as Nina sank weakly to her knees.

Rufus put on the mask. Howling with delight, Senkhara merged into his body, preparing to step into the glorious afterlife.

With a powerful rush of air, the portal on the mezzanine closed, and another portal opened on the library floor. It was as hot as a blazing furnace.

Senkhara in Rufus's body writhed in horror. "No! Nooo!"

Rufus struggled to take off the mask, but Senkhara's spirit fought him from inside. As he battled to regain his body, he stumbled over the edge of the mezzanine and tumbled, screaming, into the fiery furnace. Immediately, the portal closed, leaving nothing but the mask on the floor.

There was a moment of breathless silence. Then

Fabian rushed over to the motionless girl on the ground. "Joy! Joy!" He lifted her wrist. "I can't find a pulse."

Victor hurried to Joy's side. "Let me see. Stand back!" He checked Joy's pulse too, his face drawn with worry. "It's there. But it's very faint," he announced. He turned to Fabian. "What happened?"

Fabian gulped. "She saved me from the energy bolt that Senkhara threw at me!"

Meanwhile, Nina struggled down from the mezzanine, determined to see if Joy was okay. Amber moved to help her along the last few steps. As she reached the ground floor, the mask caught Nina's eye. At the bottom of the mask, in a shallow groove, was a single golden droplet. A tear of gold.

"Look!" called Nina weakly, picking up the mask.

Victor turned to see Nina holding the mask and pointing to the tear. "Tears of gold—the last one!" he gasped.

"It's an ingredient for the elixir, isn't it?" Nina asked.

Victor nodded. "Yes, it is. Give it to me." He paused for an agonized moment, and then seemed to come to a decision. He took the mask from Nina and tipped the golden droplet onto Joy's lips.

Joy immediately opened her eyes. "What happened?" she asked groggily.

"Stupid heroics, that's what happened," said Patricia, blinking back tears.

Fabian went to Nina, who was sitting on the bottom step, drained by her ordeal.

"Is Senkhara really gone?" she whispered.

Fabian nodded. "Yeah."

Nina rolled up her sleeve. She smiled. "My mark! It's disappeared."

Fabian checked his arm. "Mine too. I think we're all in the clear."

Nina leaned toward Fabian, and they shared a long, lingering hug.

After making sure Joy was okay, Patricia had crossed the room and was now talking to Eddie. "How did you know what to do?" she asked him.

Eddie shrugged. "I don't know. It's like someone

was telling me from inside my own head." He grinned cockily. "Rocked it, though. Right?"

Meanwhile, Alfie had picked up the mask. He removed the Frobisher gem, and it immediately reverted to ordinary bronze. Just then, Amber tapped him on the shoulder. "So, you were pretty brave today, Alfie," she said coyly.

Alfie blushed. "I know." He cleared his throat. "I've been thinking, maybe 'Amfie' does have a certain ring to it."

"I think you mean 'Alber,'" corrected Amber.

"Although I may have certain conditions," continued Alfie with a sly grin.

Amber paused, taking a deep breath. "*Aaaand* I'm calm." She smiled and linked arms with Alfie. "Let's hear them."

"Well, for starters, I'm thinking maybe matching monster masks," said Alfie, and together they made their way out of the library.

20

As Fabian and Patricia helped Joy up and began walking her to the exit, Nina gazed sympathetically at Victor. He was sitting on a chair, staring straight ahead, holding the bronze mask that Alfie had given him. He looked utterly shocked.

When everyone else had left, Nina approached Victor. "You knew what would happen to Rufus when he put on that mask, didn't you?" she asked.

Victor nodded. "Only the pure of heart may enter the afterlife and become gods. Rufus was not pure of heart."

"I think we should put the mask back where it belongs," said Nina. Victor nodded and gave it to her.

Nina cleared her throat. "I have something for you." She paused. "It's from your father." She dug into her pocket and handed Victor his father's ring.

Victor gazed in astonishment at the ring. "Where on earth . . . ?"

"He says he's sorry," Nina said gently. She put the mask back in the display case and quietly left the library as Victor looked at the ring, smiling sadly.

That evening, Anubis House was in the swing of a full-blown party. After the events in the library, Victor had agreed to a huge celebration. Amid decorations, a buffet table laden with food, and lively music, students and teachers gathered happily to eat and dance.

As the clock struck nine, Fabian went out into the hallway to find Nina descending the stairs with Amber. Nina had changed into a gorgeous yellow dress. She looked beautiful.

"Nina," Fabian breathed.

Nina stopped on the stairs, smiling down at him. Amber beamed happily, and then skipped off to join the party.

Nina continued down the stairs. As if on cue, when she reached the bottom, the music changed to a slow song. She went to Fabian under the chandelier and put her arms around him.

They started to dance, the music dimly audible from the living room. Nina rested her head on Fabian's shoulder.

"I've been thinking," murmured Fabian. "We got it all wrong, breaking up and stuff." He took a deep breath. "You do know you're the one, right?"

Nina smiled wryly. "The Chosen One?"

Fabian grinned back. "Well, *my* chosen one."

Nina leaned forward, and finally, they kissed. At that moment, Amber, Alfie, Jerome, Joy, Patricia, Eddie, Gran, and Trudy all peeked from the living room. Amber let out a loud whoop, making Nina jump.

Then Nina and Fabian laughed as Amber led a charge toward her two best friends, arms flung wide, with everyone else following close behind.